Bunjitsu Bunny's Best Move

Bunjitsu Bunny's Best Move

Written and illustrated by
John Himmelman

SQUARE
FISH

Henry Holt and Company
New York

SQUARE
FISH

An Imprint of Macmillan
175 Fifth Avenue
New York, NY 10010
mackids.com

Our books may be purchased in bulk for promotional, educational, or business use. Please
contact your local bookseller or the Macmillan Corporate and Premium Sales Department at
(800) 221-7945 ext. 5442 or by e-mail at MacmillanSpecialMarkets@macmillan.com.

Library of Congress Cataloging-in-Publication Data
Himmelman, John, author, illustrator.
[Short stories. Selections]
Bunjitsu Bunny's best move / John Himmelman.
pages   cm
Sequel to: Tales of Bunjitsu Bunny.
Summary: As Isabel, the best bunjitsu artist in her class, continues to practice her skills,
she also grows in her understanding of how to use her strongest weapon—her mind.
ISBN 978-1-250-09049-2 (paperback) · ISBN 978-0-8050-9973-7 (ebook)
[1. Martial arts—Fiction. 2. Rabbits—Fiction. 3. Animals—Fiction.] I. Title.
PZ7.H5686Bun 2015   [Fic]—dc23   2014047281

Originally published in the United States by Henry Holt and Company, LLC
First Square Fish Edition: 2016
Square Fish logo designed by Filomena Tuosto

3 5 7 9 10 8 6 4

AR: 2.8 / LEXILE: 400L

For Sofia—

may your *best move be one of many!*

Contents

Isabel

Isabel was the best bunjitsu artist in her school. She could kick higher than anyone. She could hit harder than anyone. She could throw her classmates farther than anyone.

Some were frightened of her. But Isabel never hurt another creature, unless she had to.

"Bunjitsu is not just about kicking, hitting, and throwing," she said. "It is about finding ways NOT to kick, hit, and throw."

They called her Bunjitsu Bunny.

Shadows

One day, Isabel and her brother, Max, sat in a field. "Look at our shadows on the rock," said Isabel.

"Let's see how well they know bunjitsu," said Max. Max kicked his

foot in the air. His shadow kicked
its foot in the air. Isabel blocked the
kick. Isabel's shadow blocked the
kick.

"This is fun!" said Isabel.

Max's and Isabel's shadows
fought each other.

"My shadow has big teeth!" said
Max.

Isabel laughed. "My shadow has big antlers!" she said.

"My shadow has wings and can fly!" said Max.

"My shadow can tickle your shadow so it can't fly." Isabel laughed again.

Max moved away from the rock.
His shadow grew twice as large.
"Now you have to fight a giant
bear." Max's shadow pounded
Isabel's shadow with great big paws.
Isabel's shadow fell to the ground.

"My shadow has defeated the shadow of Bunjitsu Bunny!" said Max.

Isabel stood up and walked toward the rock.

"Now your shadow is like a little mouse," said Max.

"A quick little mouse," said Isabel.

Max's shadow tried to grab her shadow. Isabel's shadow darted away. Max's shadow tried to punch Isabel's shadow. Isabel's shadow darted away. Her little shadow was too quick for Max's shadow.

"I give up," said Max. "I thought being bigger and stronger would make me win."

"Sometimes," said Isabel. "But sometimes it's better to be a little mouse than a great big bear."

Bunjitsu Bunny Fails!

One morning, Teacher said, "Practice your bunchucks, class. Tomorrow I will test you to see how good you have become."

"You don't need to practice, Isabel," said Wendy. "You never fail."

On the day of the test, all the bunjitsu students gathered in the classroom.

Kyle went first. He swung his bunchucks so fast, no one could see them. Then he knocked the ball off its stand.

"Well done!" said Teacher. "You pass."

Then it was Betsy's turn. Her
bunchucks whistled in the air and
knocked the ball off its stand.

"That is the best you have ever
done!" said Teacher. "You pass."

All the students showed Teacher what they could do. Each passed the test.

Finally, it was Isabel's turn.

"This is a waste of time," said Ben. "Of course she will pass."

"It will still be fun to watch," said Wendy.

Isabel picked up her bunchucks.

"OW!" she said when one hit her ear.

"Ooch!" she said when they got tangled around her arm.

Then she tried to knock the ball off the stand.

"Strike one," whispered Ben.

"Strike two," whispered Betsy.

"Oh no! Strike three!" whispered Kyle.

"I am sorry, Isabel," said Teacher. "You did not pass the test, but I am sure you will next time."

Isabel was very sad. She had never failed before! Teacher asked her to stay after class.

"You should not be unhappy," said Teacher.

"But everyone passed the test except me," said Isabel.

"Do you know what you did wrong?" asked Teacher.

"Yes," said Isabel.

"Can you do better?" asked Teacher.

"Yes," said Isabel.

"Lucky you," said Teacher. "They passed the test, but you learned the most."

Mountain Goat

Isabel went for a hike on a chilly winter morning. At the end of the day, it was getting cold. She took a shortcut home and came to a bridge. Mountain Goat stood in the middle.

"Hi, Mountain Goat," said Isabel. "Would you please let me pass?"

"This is my bridge," said Mountain Goat. "You can pass if you beat my mighty horns."

"I do not want to bump heads with a goat," said Isabel.

"Then swim across the icy river," said Mountain Goat.

Isabel had little choice. She backed up and got a running start. Isabel and Mountain Goat met head-to-head.

CRASH! Isabel was knocked from the bridge.

She brushed herself off and backed up even farther. They met head-to-head.

CRASH! Isabel flew backward.

"Would you like to try again?" asked Mountain Goat.

She didn't want to try again. But she did want to go home. Isabel backed up farther yet. They met head-to-head.

CRASH! Isabel landed in a far-off tree.

"The great Bunjitsu Bunny cannot beat my mighty horns," shouted Mountain Goat, laughing.

He's right, thought Isabel. "One more try," she said.

"My pleasure," said Mountain Goat.

Isabel backed up half a mile. She ran *so* fast, her body was a blur. When she reached Mountain Goat, she leapfrogged over him!

"Hey!" shouted Mountain Goat. "We were supposed to bump heads!"

"I remembered what Teacher taught me," said Bunjitsu Bunny. "Don't let your enemy choose how you will fight."

Just DO It!

Four bunnies lay in the grass,
looking up at the sky.

"That cloud looks like my
grandma," said Ben. "I wish I was
at her house right now. I love my
grandma's hugs."

"Look at the cloud next to it,"
said Wendy. "It looks like a trumpet.
I wish I had my trumpet with me. I
love making music."

"That cloud makes me think of a
kicking bunny," said Max. "I really

should practice my bunjitsu kicks some more."

Isabel stood up and left.

"Where did she go?" asked Ben.

"You never know with her," said Max.

A few hours later, Isabel returned. Her friends were still lying in the grass.

"Where were you?" asked Wendy.

"Max made me think that I should practice my bunjitsu kicks,

so I did. Wendy made me wish I could go make music, so I did. And Ben made me think of my grandma, so I went and got a nice big grandma hug."

The other three bunnies stood up.

"Where are you going?" asked
Isabel.

"You are right," said Ben. "Doing
something is better than talking
about it."

One Hundred
Squirrels

Isabel loved to bake acorn cookies. She made a batch to give to her friends. As they were cooling, Squirrel showed up.

"Are those acorn cookies?" she asked.

"Yes," said Isabel. "I would give you one, but I made just enough for my friends."

"Then I will TAKE one!" said
Squirrel. She reached for the
cookies. Isabel chased her away. But
when she turned around, Squirrel
was back.

"COOKIES!" shouted Squirrel.

"No cookies," said Isabel, and she chased Squirrel off. When she turned around, Squirrel was heading for the cookies again.

"How are you doing that?" Isabel asked. She chased Squirrel away. When she got back, Squirrel was there.

"You can't be that fast!" said Isabel.

Then another squirrel appeared. And another. And another. Soon Bunjitsu Bunny had to defeat an army of one hundred cookie-loving squirrels.

She fought them one, two,
three, ten, fifty at a time. They kept
coming back.

I can't do this all day, thought Isabel. *But I will if I have to.* Then she had an idea. She held the tray over her head.

"The first one to get to these cookies can have them all," she said.

"COOKIES!" shouted the squirrels. They were so busy fighting one another, they didn't see Isabel tiptoe away with the tray.

The next day, Isabel baked more acorn cookies. This time, she made one hundred extra.

The Climb

Isabel wanted to climb to the top of Mount Snowcap. It was the tallest mountain in the area.

"That mountain is too big," said Max. "You will never make it to the top."

"I will try," said Isabel. She grabbed her backpack and headed up the mountain.

Climb. Climb. Climb.

Up. Up. Up.

Along the way, she came across a patch of pretty pink violets. She sat and drew pictures of them.

I'd better keep going, thought Isabel, *or I will never make it to the top.*

Climb. Climb. Climb.

Up. Up. Up.

"Hello," said a voice. "You look thirsty."

"Hello," said Isabel. "I am saving my water for when I get to the top."

"I am Snowshoe Hare. Come share some sweet mountain water with me."

Isabel and Snowshoe sat and talked. He had so many stories about living on the mountain.

"I'd better get going," said Isabel,
"or I will never make it to the top."

Climb. Climb. Climb.

Up. Up. Up.

A rock bounced down the hill.
The sound echoed in the valley
below.

"Hello," called Isabel.

"Hello hello hello," called her
echo.

Isabel sang to the valley. The valley sang back to her. She was having so much fun, she lost track of time. Soon it would be dark. It was time to head down.

"Did you make it to the top?"
asked Max when she returned home.

"No," said Isabel. "But that is
okay. A goal can be something you
aim for. What happens along the
way makes it worth the try."

The Chore

One day, Teacher looked out at the garden behind the school. "There are so many weeds," he said. "Would any of you like to help get rid of them?"

All the students volunteered.

"I think it is a lesson he is teaching us," said Isabel. "Pulling weeds makes us practice the bunjitsu elbow strike."

"I think he wants us to dig them with our paws," said Ben. "It makes us practice the bunjitsu tornado block."

"No," said Kyle. "He wants us to use our feet to practice our bunjitsu kicks."

The bunnies spent the rest of
the day in the garden. They pulled.
They dug. They kicked. When they
were done, Teacher came outside.

"The garden looks wonderful," he said.

"And watch this," said Isabel. She showed Teacher her bunjitsu elbow strike.

"Good, good," said Teacher.

"Look at my bunjitsu tornado block," said Ben. His paws circled through the air.

"Beautiful," said Teacher.

"Watch THIS!" said Kyle. He kicked mightily in the air.

"Very nice," said Teacher.

All the bunnies showed Teacher
what he'd had them practice.

"Those were good lessons you taught us," said Isabel.

"You taught yourselves those lessons," said Teacher.

"But isn't that why you wanted us to weed the garden?" she asked.

"No," said Teacher. "Sometimes the garden just needs to be weeded."

Lynx

Isabel was hopping home from school. Lynx blocked her path.

"So you are the great Bunjitsu Bunny," he said. "If I beat you in a fight, everyone will be afraid of ME!"

"I do not want to fight you," said Isabel.

"Too bad!" said Lynx. He leapt at Isabel. The two fought until she held him to the ground.

"Now it's over," said Isabel. "No more fighting."

The next day, Lynx was waiting
for her.

"I will beat you today," he said.
He leapt at the bunny. The two
fought until Isabel held him to the
ground.

"No more fighting," she said.

Lynx did not listen. Every day, he waited for Isabel. Every day, he fought her. Every day, he lost.

"I will keep fighting you until I win," said Lynx.

"Is there any way I can get you to stop?" asked Isabel.

"No one can make me do anything," said Lynx.

Isabel thought a moment.

"Okay," she said. "One more fight."

Lynx leapt at Isabel. The bunny fell to the ground.

"You win," she said. "I give up."

"I defeated Bunjitsu Bunny,"
he roared, and ran back into the
woods.

Kyle walked by. "Why did you let Lynx beat you?" he asked.

"I would rather lose one little fight," said Isabel, "than win a thousand of them."

Your Best Move

Bunjitsu class was over for the day. "Before you go home," said Teacher, "I want each of you to show me your best way to stop a fight."

"I have a good one," said Betsy.

"Max, come and attack me."

Max ran at Betsy.

"WAHAA!" shouted Betsy. She
flipped Max through the air!

"My turn," said Max. "Betsy, come and attack me."

Betsy ran at Max.

"YAHEE!" shouted Max. He wrestled Betsy to the ground!

"I've got one," said Wendy. "Kyle, attack!"

Kyle leapt at Wendy.

"HEEYIP!" shouted Wendy. She pulled his ears!

"Watch this," said Kyle. "Wendy, ATTACK!"

"HOOBAWOOBA!" shouted Kyle. He spun and sent Wendy flying!

"Now it's my turn," said Ben.
"Isabel, ATTACK!"

Isabel grabbed Ben's shirt.
"HEEYA!" shouted Ben. He
yanked her to the ground!

When it was Isabel's turn, everyone backed up. They were all afraid to attack Bunjitsu Bunny.

"Be brave, my bunnies," said Teacher. No one stepped forward.

"Okay," said Betsy. "I will attack Isabel."

Betsy ran at Isabel.

Isabel wrapped her arms around Betsy and gave her a hug.

"This is my favorite way to stop a fight," she said.

"I'll attack her," said Wendy.

"No, me," said Max.

"No, I will," said Kyle.

"Next," said Ben.

"Nothing is more powerful than the bunjitsu hug," said Teacher with a laugh.

Mole Hole

Isabel liked to sit in her
underground den. Her friend Mole
often visited her. They sipped
blueberry juice. They shared funny
stories.

Sometimes they just sat quietly
and enjoyed being together.

One day, Mole looked sad.

"What is wrong?" asked Isabel.

"I always visit your den," said
Mole, "but you never visit mine."

"I would love to visit your den," said Isabel.

"Follow me," said Mole. He disappeared into his tunnel.

Mole's tunnel was very small.
Isabel barely squeezed through.
When she got to the end, she could
hardly move. She popped her head
into Mole's den.

"It is a very nice place," said
Isabel, "but I cannot fit inside."

"Oh," said Mole. "I did not think
of that."

He showed Isabel his favorite things. "This is a picture of my mom and dad."

"This is my comfy mushroom seat."

"This is the flute I like to play."

"I wish I could join you," said Isabel.

The next day, Isabel was very
busy. She drew a picture. She went
hunting in the damp forest. Then she
found a stick to carve.

"Come on over," she called to
Mole through his tunnel.

Mole came to Isabel's den.
Waiting inside was a comfy
mushroom seat, a flute, and a
picture of his mom and dad.

"That looks just like them!" said
Mole.

"Now my den is your den, too!"
said Isabel.

Mole perched on his comfy
mushroom seat and played a happy
tune.

Bzzzzz

Isabel watched Dragonfly zipping over a pond. "How did you learn to fly?" she asked.

"It is easy," said Dragonfly. "You just need four long wings and a long body."

Bzzzzz . . . Bumblebee buzzed
past.

"She doesn't have four long wings
and a long body," said Isabel.

b z z z z z

"Hmm," said Dragonfly.

Butterfly landed on a flower below. "You don't need four long wings and a long body," she said.

b z z z z z z z

"You need four WIDE wings and a TINY body."

Bzzzzz . . . Bumblebee buzzed by.

"She doesn't have four wide
wings and a tiny body," said Isabel.
"Hmm," said Butterfly.

Z Z Z Z Z Z Z Z Z Z Z Z Z

bzzzz zzzz

Raven landed on a branch above. "You don't need four wide wings and a tiny body," he said. "You need TWO wings covered in FEATHERS."

Bzzzz . . . Bumblebee buzzed past.

"She doesn't have two wings covered in feathers," said Isabel.

"Hmm," said Raven.

Bzzzzz . . . Bumblebee buzzed back and forth between the reeds.

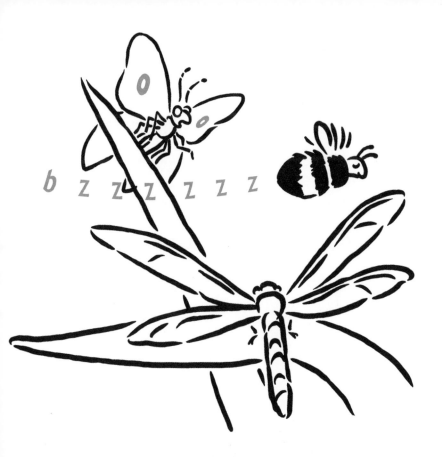

"That does not make sense," said
Dragonfly. "Bumblebee has very
short wings."

"And a large, round body," said
Butterfly.

"And no feathers," said Raven.
"You can't fly with short wings
and a large, round body," they said.
"Maybe you can," said Isabel, "if
you don't know you cannot."

b z z z z z z z z

Paper Bunny

Isabel and her friends were making paper animals.

Wendy made a paper goldfish.

Kyle made a paper bear.

Ben made a paper penguin.

Isabel made a paper mouse.

"Who can make a paper bunny?"
asked Wendy.

Ben folded a piece of paper. "No, this looks like a frog," he said.

Kyle folded a piece of paper.
"This is a bunny with no ears," he
said.

Wendy folded a piece of paper.
"This is ears with no bunny," she
said.

"Isabel," said Ben, "you are good at this. Will you show us how to make a paper bunny?"

"Yes," said Isabel. "But I can't show you now."

A week went by. "Can you show us how to make a paper bunny?" asked Wendy.

"Yes," said Isabel. "But I can't show you now."

Another week went by. "Now can you show us how to make a paper bunny?" asked Ben.

"Soon," said Isabel.

One month later, everyone was in
Isabel's room. "NOW can you show
us how to make a paper bunny?"
they asked.

Isabel took out a piece of paper. Her paws moved quickly. Fold. Fold. Fold. Fold. Fold. Fold. She held up a perfect paper bunny!

"You did that so quickly! Why did you make us wait so long?" asked Wendy.

Isabel walked across her room
and opened her closet door. Out fell
hundreds of practice paper bunnies.

How to Make a Bunny Face

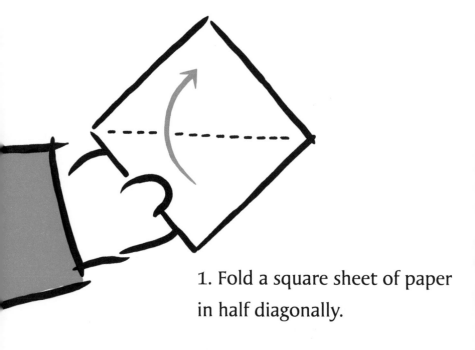

1. Fold a square sheet of paper in half diagonally.

2. Fold triangle in half, make a crease, and unfold.

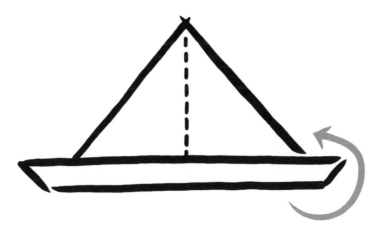

3. Fold up a little of the bottom.

4. Fold the
bottom corners
up to the crease.

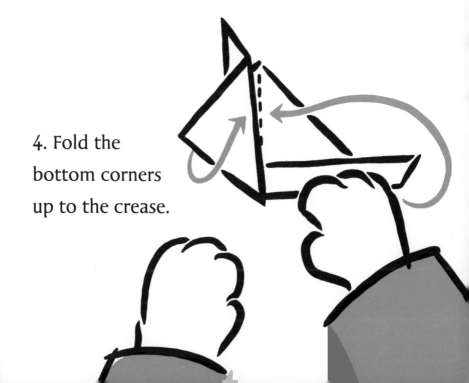

5. Flip it over.

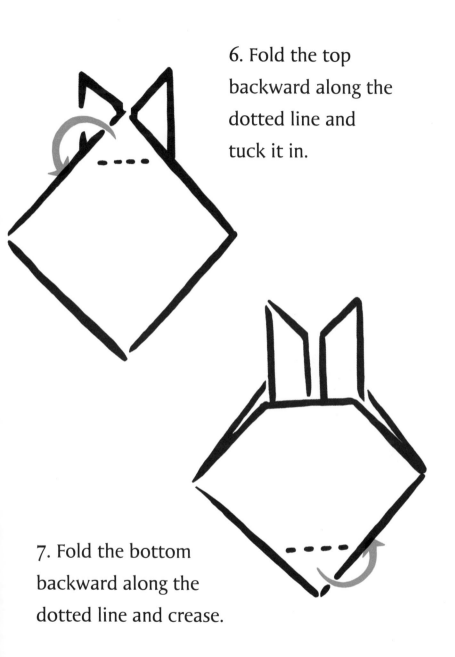

6. Fold the top backward along the dotted line and tuck it in.

7. Fold the bottom backward along the dotted line and crease.

8. Draw a bunny face!

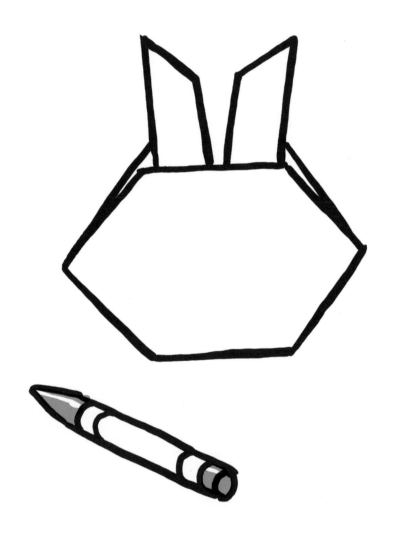

The Bunjitsu Code

All Bunjitsu students must do their best to follow the rules of Bunjitsu. If you wish to learn this art, you must read this and sign your name at the bottom.

I promise to:

- Practice my art until I am good at it. And then keep practicing.

- Never start a fight.

- Do all I can to avoid a fight.

- Help those who need me.

- Study the world.

- Learn from those who know more than I do.

- Share what I love.

- Find what makes me laugh, and laugh loudly. And often.

- Make someone smile every day.

- Keep my body strong and healthy.

- Try things that are hard for me to do.

GOFISH

JOHN HIMMELMAN

What did you want to be when you grew up?
In order from kindergarten to high school: scientist, entomologist, veterinarian, cartoonist.

When did you realize you wanted to be a writer?
I always enjoyed writing stories and drawing pictures. I honestly cannot think back on a time when I didn't!

What's your favorite childhood memory?
Playing outside with my friends and brothers on summer evenings. There was no school the next morning, so we'd stay out past dark—under the streetlights along our little dead-end road. It was such an exciting new world. Maybe that's why I enjoy exploring and writing about the nature found at night.

As a young person, who did you look up to most?
Besides my parents, my uncle Roland. He was a soldier who came to live with us when he returned from the Vietnam War. I have two younger brothers, but he was like an older brother to me.

 SQUARE FISH

What was your favorite thing about school?
Art class! It was always the highlight of my day. I was lucky to have very encouraging art teachers throughout my school years. And we got to listen to music during class.

What were your hobbies as a kid? What are your hobbies now?
I was really into bugs. I used to collect all different kinds and keep them in jars in my room. I'd study them for hours and hours, often drawing them. Now? I practice martial arts, play guitar, watch birds, chase butterflies, look for excuses to get together with friends, and . . . I collect all different kinds of bugs and keep them in jars in my room. I study them for hours and hours, often drawing them.

Did you play sports as a kid?
My dad would organize games for all the kids on our block. We played baseball, basketball, and football—depending on the season. I also played Little League baseball and CYO basketball.

What was your first job, and what was your "worst" job?
My first job was as a paperboy, delivering *Newsday* on my bicycle after school. It was also my worst job! I pedaled that overloaded bike through all kinds of weather every day of the week. Sundays were the worst! I had to get up at 5:00 a.m. to assemble the ad-bloated newspapers and then head out in two or three trips to deliver them. BUT, I made enough money to buy a new ten-speed bike and a camping tent!

What book is on your nightstand now?
There's never just one. *The Inflationary Universe* by Alan H. Guth (I love space stuff!); *Love and Hate in Jamestown: John Smith, Pocahontas, and the Start of a New Nation* by David A. Price (I love

history stuff); *Jun Fan/Jeet Kune Do, The Textbook* by Chris Kent and Tim Tackett (I love martial arts stuff); and *The Ruby Knight* by David Eddings (I love fantasy). I'm also hooked on *The Walking Dead* and other comics, but they get read too fast to make it to my nightstand.

How did you celebrate publishing your first book?
I had just graduated from college (School of Visual Arts), having had my first book (*Talester the Lizard*) accepted by a publisher. I bought a 1980 Subaru Brat and drove cross-country from my then-home in New York to California. The celebrations of books to follow never matched that first one.

Where do you write your books?
I usually sit at a big desk in my studio, surrounded by snoring dogs and a chirping cat. Just to my right is a big window to my garden, meadow, and wooded yard. It could be said that I spend too much time staring out that window, but I'd disagree. Sometimes I give in to the call of the outdoors and move outside to write. Many of the Bunjitsu Bunny stories were written while sitting on a wooded shore by a big lake.

What sparked your imagination for the Bunjitsu Bunny series?
When I opened my martial arts school (with fellow author Ed Ricciuti), a local paper did a story on us. The reporter featured one of our talented Hapkido students, eight-year-old Isabel. I shared the article with Kate Farrell, my editor at Holt, who then urged me to write a story about a girl who is an exceptional martial artist. I made the girl a bunny, created the art of "bunjitsu," and a world was born. The thirteen tales in this book are gleaned from lessons I have learned in martial arts and in life.

All the names of the characters in the book are or were students in our school. The signatures on the Bunjitsu Code in the back are the actual handwriting of each of those students!

SQUARE FISH

Do you know how to do martial arts?
I practice and teach Hapkido and Jeet Kune Do at my school, Green Hill Martial Arts, in Killingworth, Connecticut. We recently moved into a building built in 1881 that was once the town's meeting place for farmers, and then our old town hall. I love it there! I feel like we've become part of our town's long history!

What is your favorite thing about Isabel?
Isabel is very comfortable with who she is—so much so, she doesn't feel the need to prove her talents to others. But as skilled as she is, she's not perfect. She finds joy in conquering her challenges and learning new things.

What is more difficult for you: the writing process or the illustration process?
It depends on the book. The art for *Bunjitsu Bunny's Best Move* is done in a looser style than I've used in the past. It is sometimes hard for me to say to myself, "STOP! Put down your brush! The picture is finished!"

What challenges do you face in the writing process, and how do you overcome them?
In the thirty-something years I've been doing this, I still don't know if what I write will be of interest to others. I keep telling myself it shouldn't matter, but if you make a living as a writer/illustrator, it kinda does. . . . I still try to write for myself, though, and just hope that afterward there will be someone out there who will enjoy reading it.

What is your favorite word?
Betsy. It's attached to my wife.

If you could live in any fictional world, what would it be?
I don't think there's a fictional world that can match the one I'm living in now.

Who is your favorite fictional character?
Gandalf the Grey.

What was your favorite book when you were a kid?
The King with Six Friends by Jay Williams, illustrated by Imero Gobbato.

If you could travel in time, where would you go and what would you do?
I sure would love to see some dinosaurs.

What's the best advice you have ever received about writing?
Fellow children's book author Kay Kudlinski always says, "Writers write!" So many people think about someday writing that story they always imagined they would write. Real writers don't think about it; they do it.

What advice do you wish someone had given you when you were younger?
"John, pay more attention in history class. You'll have less catching up to do when you realize there are no better stories than those of the people and events of our past."

Do you ever get writer's block? What do you do to get back on track?
I do. The best way to break through that wall is to write your way through it.

What do you want readers to remember about your books?
I want them to look at the faces in the pictures and know that as I was drawing every expression, I was wearing that same expression on my face. It's something I was told I do.

 SQUARE FISH

What would you do if you ever stopped writing?
I would find other ways to share stories, but writing is still the most comfortable way for me to do so.

If you were a superhero, what would your superpower be?
It comes down to the choice of being indestructible, invisible, or able to fly. Which would allow me the greatest advantage as a true force of good in this world? I tend to lean toward invisibility, but would not whine too loudly if either of the other two powers was bestowed upon me.

Do you have any strange or funny habits?
I sometimes pat my car and say "thank you" after getting home from a long trip. After years of doing this I found out that my grandfather used to do the same thing.

What do you consider to be your greatest accomplishment?
When asked this question, many people say their children. My son, Jeff, and daughter, Lizzie, however, are gifts, not accomplishments. So I'd say that finding a way to make a living that keeps me growing and learning, that satisfies my unrelenting need to create is a pretty big accomplishment.

What will this bunjitsu master get up to next?

Keep reading for a sneak peek!

The Floating Rabbit

"I have a new challenge for you," said Teacher to his bunjitsu students. He pointed to two hoops on the floor, one on either side of the room.

"Each of you has to take a turn standing in one circle."

"That's too easy," said Wendy.

"And," continued Teacher, "you must move across the room to the other circle without touching the floor."

"Rabbits can't float," said Ben.

"No, but we can jump," said Max.
He stepped inside the hoop and ran
in circles to build up speed. Then
he leapt in the air, toward the other
circle.

He didn't even come close.

"Me next," said Kyle. He picked up a long stick and entered the circle.

"WAHOOOOOO!" shouted Kyle, and he pole-vaulted toward the other circle.

He didn't even come close.

Ben took his turn. He sat in the circle. He sat and sat and sat.

"Well?" asked Betsy.

"I'm thinking," said Ben.

"You can think outside the circle," said Betsy. "Let us try."

Hmmm, thought Isabel. *Think outside the circle. . . .*

Soon it was her turn. Bunjitsu Bunny sat in the circle.

"Kyle and Betsy, will you please
do me a favor?"

"Of course," they said.

"Will you carry me over to the
other circle?"

Everyone laughed as Isabel was
carried across the room. They set
her down inside the other circle.

"Well done," said Teacher. "What did you learn?"

"Sometimes," said Isabel, "friends can help us do things we cannot do on our own."

Follow along with Isabel
on all her adventures!

Read the
whole series!